The Topless Tower

# The Topless Tower

Silvina Ocampo

Translated by James Womack

Hesperus Worldwide

Hesperus Worldwide
Published by Hesperus Press Limited
4 Rickett Street, London SW6 1RU
www.hesperuspress.com

*The Topless Tower* first published in Spanish as *La torre sin fin* in 1968

This translation first published by Hesperus Press Limited, 2010



Work published within the framework of 'Sur' Translation Support Program of the Ministry of Foreign Affairs, International Trade and Worship of the Argentine Republic.

Designed and typeset by Fraser Muggeridge studio
Printed in Jordan by Jordan National Press

ISBN: 978-1-84391-855-4

# Contents

# Introduction

There seems to be no clear reason for Silvina Ocampo to be less well known in the English-speaking world than the other two Argentinian writers with whom she is most often associated, Adolfo Bioy Casares and Jorge Luis Borges, unless it be the highly private stance she adopted towards her writing. It is part of the legend of Silvina Ocampo that she was a perfectionist: in the popular imagination there are ample gaps between her collections of short stories and poetry. This is untrue, and a glance at her bibliography should put this notion to rest for good: hers is the sort of perfectionism that results some years in two poetry collections, two books of stories (she published nine books in the 1970s alone).

However, it is the case that the slim volume that follows is one of only two novels published during Ocampo's lifetime, the other being a detective story written with her husband, Bioy Casares (a book with the slightly worrying title for a husband-and-wife collaboration of *Los que aman, odian*, or *Those Who Love Also Hate*). Demons, doubles, Lewis Carroll's Alice, paintings that come to life... these form the skeleton – one would not dare to call it the 'structure' – of Ocampo's surrealist farce, a fairy-tale-ish work which honours not only Carroll, but Victorian nonsense literature in general, as well as a whole international host of other writers and genres, from Lenora Carrington to Ana María Matute. At the same time, *The Topless Tower* (*La torre sin fin* in the original Spanish) defiantly shows off Ocampo's own personal manner of looking into the world and reinterpreting it for her readers.

It is not surprising that painting and drawing are part of – in many ways the motor for – the magical world inside the tower. For a long period of her life Ocampo dedicated herself exclusively to painting. And yet she needed to find other means of expressing the worlds of her imagination. In 1934, the same year that she met Bioy Casares, Ocampo co-founded a puppet company, 'La Sirena', that performed versions of classical fairy tales in Buenos Aires. It is unclear if the call to write came specifically from this experience in retelling well-known stories and, along with the rest of the troupe, giving physical form to sets and characters she had thought up. However, when she turned to writing, Ocampo, as is perhaps to be expected in someone with a long training as a visual artist, adopted a wide number of forms. She did not only write stories 'for children' (something she invested a great deal of time in after adopting Marta, her husband's daughter), she also wrote plays (only one of these, *The Magical Dog*, was staged in her lifetime), and she went as far as proposing a collection of retellings of world fairy tales to the publisher Emecé. Unfortunately this volume never appeared; one would have liked to see which stories formed the primordial cultural soup for such a highly imaginative writer.

The outline of Ocampo's personal life is well known, although it is both a surprise and a shame that no full-length biography of her yet exists in either Spanish or English. Born in 1903 into a talented family (her sister Victoria became a significant figure in the Latin American publishing world), Silvina Ocampo was married to Adolfo Bioy Casares, a magnificent author in his own right, but largely famous nowadays as Jorge Luis Borges's closest collaborator; she raised a family and happily adopted a mother's role; she maintained important friendships with a number of authors, including Italo Calvino; she kept writing, never questioning the needs of her portentous imagination. She developed new ways of connecting images and texts, and wrote stories where pictures and words, the perceived and the imagined and the real, all combine to create new worlds or help us understand our own. But one more answer to the question of why Silvina Ocampo is not better known is that large parts of her activity, her highly imaginative stories and plays and poetry, has to be filtered, or so it seems, through the unfairly marginalising label of 'children's writing'.

Ocampo never really drew a distinction between writing for children and for adults. 'Crossover' literature is not a category that the prodigious output of the last decade – Philip Pullman's *Northern Lights*, J.K. Rowling's Harry Potter saga – has invented for itself. Crossover literature has existed since before J.R.R. Tolkien and C.S. Lewis, has its first stirrings as far back as authors such as Arthur Ransome, writers who can be read and reread by adults in search of the same escapist pleasures they experienced as children. Ocampo sees no need to write within set conventions: the same goes for her disdain of preordained categories. In the only anthology of her writing that she herself selected, distinctions between different genres are non-existent, and she does not categorise her different texts 'as' specific types of writing. In this she follows other Latin American authors (the so-called 'magical realists' are the most obvious example) who derive their inspiration from fantasy or the Gothic alongside more canonical literature. For Ocampo, as for Julio Cortázar or Gabriel García Márquez, every single event, high or low, childish or adult, can be seen as useful material for writing.

Ocampo's refusal to categorise is highly illuminating. Her writing 'for children' never ceases to address her interlocutors as grown-ups would do, while the speech of her child-heroes reflects the unarguable 'logic' of children's discussion. Ocampo's work allows us a glimpse into the child's mind of such a rare truthfulness that it almost seems as if she has recorded, verbatim, a casual conversation between two pre-adolescents. Other signs alert us to her deep understanding of a child's universe, as well as her ignoring the usual characteristics of 'children's literature' in her pursuit of a deeper likeness: Leandro, the hero of *The Topless Tower*, alternates between the first and the third person, 'like some famous [i.e. grown-up] writers'. He dutifully underlines all the words he uses whose meaning he does not know: another attempt to be taken seriously by the reader, to be judged beyond his years. Such subtle signs help articulate with rare accuracy what it means for a child to be a child. The same goes for the timelessness of the whole adventure: it is only by the occasional mention of a computer or a robot or television that we have any clear idea of what century Leandro is living in. The story reproduces a child's solipsism. Above all, *The Topless Tower* is an allegory of reaching maturity, of obtaining certain lessons which are indispensable to the development of our minds (it is another of Ocampo's great skills that such lessons are never patronising, never moralising): it is not, for example, surprising that the number of underlined words declines as we reach the end of the novel, where Leandro leaves his thoughtless younger self behind.

Leandro regularly claims to be fighting against the Devil in the tower. It is the Devil, we are led to believe, who has imprisoned him and becomes his major adversary. However, we cannot ascertain if the Devil is real or a figment of his precocious imaginings: Leandro himself (a little like Max in Maurice Sendak's *Where the Wild Things Are*) dresses as the Devil for Carnival: 'It's the cheapest costume there is.' The reader is never fully aware of where the boundaries lie between reality and imagination, between the sacred and the profane, between painting and colours and images and their textual description. The topless tower is itself a boundary-space, where previously hard and fast rules and categories are shown to be vague and uncertain. For the duration of the novel, we are completely immersed in a child's universe, which is emphatically not the same as a universe conceived simply for children. This is the great achievement of *The Topless Tower*: to force the adult reader, in a certain measure, to enter into the thoughts and hopes of this lost and alien world.

*James and Marian Womack, 2010*

# The Topless Tower

## The Topless Tower

A long time ago, or else not so very long ago, I couldn't say, summer held out its green leaves, its mirrors of sky-blue water, the fruits in the trees. The days were not long enough: I could never finish swimming, or rowing, or eating chocolate, or painting with the watercolours from my black paintbox. I'd got prizes from school, but I am disobedient. I imitate people, like monkeys do. I even imitate the way people write. Like some famous writers, I use the first and third persons simultaneously. My parents have a lot of books. Sometimes I can't understand what I write, it's so well written, but I can always guess what I wanted to say. I'll underline the words I don't understand. Someone once said to me, and I suspect it was the Devil, 'The great writers are those who don't understand what they write; the others are worthless.'

One afternoon I was playing with my friends among the pines and cedars in our garden when a man, dressed in black with a black bowler hat and a moustache painted on his face, appeared at the garden gate. He spoke in French; every now and then he would, with the aid of a book, drop in a few words of English, or German, or Italian. He must have been very rich, because he had on his little finger a gold ring, mounted with a ruby, but at the same time he seemed tattered and dirty, like an old and battered piece of furniture. He was carrying a valise and a few large brown-paper parcels. After ceremoniously greeting my mother, who sat knitting under a tree, he opened one of these parcels like a conjuror and took out a few canvases that he leaned against the half-open iron gate. He opened the valise and took out some more pictures, and lined them up against the fence. The pictures were horrible. I wouldn't say that they were clumsily painted, but they were absurd. A cold light illuminated them. The first picture was of a sketchy yellow tower, windowless and covered in stains. The second one was of a room full of rustic wooden furniture. There was a desolate magnificence in the unlit golden candelabras, in the porcelain jug, in the silver bedframe with its canopy. The remaining pictures were of other, sadder, more lugubrious rooms. The last one I looked at was of a huge studio with an easel in the middle; to one side, on a decorated table supported by carved golden dragons, were all kinds of brushes and paints and paper and canvas, palettes and flasks. I laughed. The more I looked at the paintings, the more I laughed. My mother took me by the hand and spoke into my ear.

'I've told you not to laugh at people.'

I carried on laughing. They both looked at me: the man with distaste, my mother with sadness. I looked down at the ant-covered ground, lowering my head to hide my giggles. I tried to imitate the man behind his back. He spoke to my mother in his fluting voice.

'Madam, would you like to buy a painting? Oil, pastel, acrylic? Which do you prefer?'

I burst out laughing again, because I thought he had said 'pasta', and because I saw he'd forgotten to put the windows in any of his paintings. My mother answered smoothly.

'They must be very expensive, and I'm afraid we don't have the money to pay for them.'

'These ones are oil paintings, madam. Your son thinks I don't know how to paint windows. How old is he?'

She replied quickly, but with the same smoothness.

'He's eight, sir.'

'Don't fib. You, child, are nine years old. Can't you see the wrinkle on his forehead?' He looked at me closely. 'What are you called? Well, can't you speak?'

'Leandro.' My mother's voice trembled as she pronounced my name, and then she added, 'Why do you ask?'

'I'm interested in the names of devils, and mongrels.'

'No, please sir,' my mother said, 'that's not respectful. Don't say that.'

'You think so little of the Devil?'

Swift as lightning, or a conjuror, the man spun round and caught me imitating him. Would to God and all His angels I had never done so. I heard his fluting voice again.

'I paint like this both deliberately and obliquely,' he said, looking at me.

'What does it mean, deliberately and obliquely?' I asked.

'Look it up in the dictionary when you get the chance,' he replied. 'A boy of your age can't be ignorant.'

'I'm not ignorant,' I protested.

'It doesn't matter what you are,' he said, turning very pale. 'These pictures are of my buildings. I am faithful to reality; I am honest.'

He cracked these last words out from between his purple lips. He stroked my head hypocritically and I heard a buzzing noise in my ears.

The garden, my mother, my friends, the man dressed in black, the pictures lined up against the fence… all of these disappeared, and I found myself inside a tower, the tower from the pictures, with its lugubrious rooms. Luckily enough, I still had my boxing gloves, my bag and the water flask I usually took on picnics. I had been invited to one that very afternoon. They'd be waiting for me. I took a sip of water. I looked unsuccessfully on the wall for a window I could use to escape, or from which I could call to my friends to come and help me. I slowly opened a door: what would be waiting for me on the other side? Hell? An abyss? Would I fall into a pit full of rats and vipers and wishes, as in the fairy tales, or else into a pit full of silence and cold and darkness, like they have in science fiction stories? Darkness surrounded me. I felt scared and took a step backwards. I went into another room: the walls were white with large grey patches, and it was full of rustic wooden furniture. There was a desolate magnificence in the unlit golden candelabras, in the porcelain jug, in the silver bedframe with its canopy.

Fear made me hungry: I hunted in my pocket for a bar of chocolate my mother had given me and greedily ate half. Had I already become resigned to the idea of finding no windows? I opened another door, slowly, and entered another room, as ugly as the one that had preceded it. I observed a few differences: the bedframes were made of green iron, with no mattresses, but with thick red bedspreads covered in red flowers that waved in an invisible wind. Where could the wind come from if there were no windows? A wardrobe stretched its rough sides up to the ceiling; a small rocking chair caught my attention with its continuous back-and-forth.

What to do now? I left the room to look for a window. Could it really be possible that I had not seen any windows? I'd make a useless detective! A detective is never tricked. I don't want to be a ridiculous detective, someone who doesn't know what he's looking for. This tower is treacherous as the Devil. How could I think that there were no windows that opened onto landscapes to escape over? The tower could be omnipotent, with invisible windows that appeared and disappeared depending on the time of day. I won't give up, and hope to find something of supreme importance, something no one could find apart from me. I will find something as soon as possible: here we are, here, a black space in the rectangular wall denoted a window. He approached it and, with some disgust, put his head through. Complete darkness blinded him. He pulled back terrified, feeling as if he were about to fall into the void.

Had I gone through all the stages of terror yet? Had my curiosity been aroused? Had this tower, these rooms that all seemed ghost-ridden, handed me over to silence and darkness? Maybe I would find a window in one of the corridors I hadn't yet passed along. I kept on through the tower's interminable rooms and corridors. How cynical chance can be: I had always wanted to live in a tower. What did cynical actually mean?

Hopefully, I opened a door that was taller than the others. I entered a huge studio. It had an easel ready with a canvas in the middle; to one side, on a decorated table supported by carved golden dragons, were all kinds of brushes and paints and paper and canvas, palettes and flasks. I remembered Mr Devil's horrible painting. The dragons' feet seemed to move, but they stopped when I looked at them. I examined the room thoroughly: there was no other door, and no windows. Had I really seen the whole inside of the tower, which was immense and yet as small as the lift in my house? Whenever it stopped between floors, I always thought that I would suffocate within its creaking wooden walls. What would I do if gardens no longer existed? In fear, I picked up a few brushes and felt them. I picked up the palette, the most important thing, with even more fear. When nothing unpleasant happened, I opened some tubes of paint and squeezed them onto the palette. I stood in front of the easel and started to paint. To begin with I found it impossible to spread the paint onto the canvas; little by little, using a liquid that I found in a bottle, I overcame this problem. If I had been able to paint the garden at my house, and the greenhouses, and the river where I used to bathe, and my mother knitting under a tree, then I would have been all right, but when I finished the painting after a great deal of effort I found that I had painted a sketchy yellow tower.

I had painted a window, but so badly that it only showed a little piece of sky. I consoled myself by thinking that at least I would be able to see a star in the night, or, with a great deal of luck, the moon. I did not notice the miracle that had taken place. I won't deny it: absent-mindedness is a fault of mine. 'People do not always notice miracles,' my mother says. The light did not change. Was it day or night? I did not know. I had never cared about the time, and had only ever appreciated clocks made out of chocolate, but now I worried that it was getting late. Day and night do not exist in a building with no windows or doors. I carried on painting in order to forget such a horrible thought, that dinner-time would never come, nor playtime, nor my birthday. More than anything I wanted to paint my mother as I had last seen her, knitting under a tree: the gate, the garden, the hedge. With great difficulty I spread paint onto the canvas. When I had finished my painting and stood back in order to look at it, I saw that I had painted one of the ugly rooms of my prison. Disheartened, I decided to stop painting. I took a pencil and started to write these pages on some sketching paper. At home they always used to tell me that I wrote like an adult. They used the word erudite. Of course, they then added with slight distaste, 'You spend a lot of time with books and grown-ups'. I went back to look at my other paintings. In one of the angles of the ceiling I had drawn, I noticed a little branch I had not seen before; so, a tiny part at least existed of the landscape I had wanted to paint. I felt so happy when I saw this branch that I involuntarily reached out to touch its leaves. They seemed so real, with the little shadows that hemmed their edges. It was with astonishment that I discovered that the branch was indeed real. I took it in my hands and breathed in the smell of the foliage, something I had not done for a long time.

With new hope, I started to paint another picture. I suspected that the objects that appeared would become real, like the branch: my efforts were inspired by fear and curiosity. I tried to paint the river where I used to swim, with the great willows on its banks and the sailing boats passing like butterflies. When I finished the painting, I saw that I had painted another one of the ugly rooms of my prison. However, I was happy when I found a large branch, much larger than the previous one, a cedar branch, with a seedpod that looked like a spider. I rushed to touch it; I picked it up and let it fall in horror: a spider, one of the ones my cousin calls a 'chicken', came out from the leaves and fell to the floor, where it looked at me attentively. I screamed. How long was it since I had heard my own voice? It must have been a long time, because I thought I was hearing someone else's voice. I tiptoed back towards the door, and the spider followed me. I have never been scared of spiders, but this time I was terrified. Something about its eyes warned me that it was not of this earth. As bravely as I could, fearing that my life was in danger, I tried to stamp on it. It felt elastic and resistant as a cushion underfoot, and I felt it lifting me imperceptibly off the floor. 'You won't kill me like this,' it said with a groan. I jerked my foot away and ran out before the spider could spring at me. I shut the door.

I ran through the rooms and shut all the doors behind me. I didn't think that a single door would be enough to save me from this monster. The minutes passed very slowly. I had never felt so scared, not even on the darkest nights. I heard something creak, or at least I thought I did. I pressed my ear to the keyhole. Little by little, my distress and worry turned back into bravery. I opened the door slowly; I was as uncertain but more scared than the first time. I went into the contiguous room. I went from room to room opening all the doors. When I reached the last one I stopped and looked around for some object that I might be able to use as a weapon. There was nothing. I could have drawn one, made it real. The thought didn't occur to me. I sat down by the door and tried to calm myself down. I had to go back into the room. I had to paint. If I did not, then I would be accepting my defeat. I opened the door.

Everything was in its place; the paintings were intact. Impatiently, I picked up the brushes again. I tried to paint the creeper-covered trees in the garden of my house; the fountain with its eight fishes; the walnut tree in whose trunk I hid myself during siesta time; an orange tree, covered in oranges and blossom. The creepers were so twisted that they looked like snakes. Nobody could know how much this painting cost me. When I finished it I saw I had painted the enormous studio. The easel was leaning against a twisted creeper. I pulled the creeper straight. It was covered in strong-scented flowers. I shut my eyes and smelt them, imagining myself back in the garden. It was exactly like being outside, in the open air under the trees at home. If I could have prolonged this moment, then I would have been happy. I opened my eyes; I thought I had sensed a foreign presence in the room. I saw a snake coiled on the floor. My mother and I together had often looked up in dictionaries or books about natural science the distinguishing features of poisonous snakes, but at that moment I could not remember if it was gaboon vipers that were the worst ones. The snake wound and unwound feverishly: it was either looking for a way out through the skirting board or else was trying to approach me obliquely. Suddenly it reared up its head and looked straight at me. Where was the spider? Maybe they would have got into a fight and left me alone. But the snake, manoeuvring its way across the room and calling my name, *Lean dro*, as if it were two names, headed for the door.

'Same to you!' I shouted at it.

I shut the door and left it outside.

Suddenly, I noticed that I had playfully added a bird and a monkey to the unfinished window I had painted. To my great surprise, when the window became real, so did the two little animals. I called the monkey Iris and the bird Bamboo. I offered them water for refreshment; they drank thirstily. It was as if we were in a circus. I ordered them to walk and they walked; I ordered them to dance, and they danced. Also, when I asked them to chatter more loudly or more quietly, they obeyed me admirably. I fed them with meat and birdseed. To start with, I didn't know how to draw the meat or the birdseed, or the lettuce which I thought would make a balanced diet, but it all turned out all right, even though the grains of seed were larger than normal, the meat was more tender, and the lettuce more clumpy. Using old newspapers, I made aeroplanes like my uncle the papyrologist had taught me, and had a great deal of fun. I had an idea, a fairly childish one: when I got out of this prison I would perform in a circus, because nobody before me had had the idea of training such a strange pair, a bird and a monkey.

Bamboo's job was to chase the paper aeroplanes as they flew, and Iris's was to bring them back. Ambition can be deadly. People had told me this, but now I was given proof of this proverb that I had heard so many times and to which I had paid no attention. I made a very special paper aeroplane, one that could fly further than the others and swoop down very fast.

With the aeroplane in my hand I stood next to the window, my attempt at a window; Iris and Bamboo were right by me, alert with expectation. As soon as I threw the aeroplane, Bamboo launched herself into the air like an acrobat. Iris held back for a few moments as if paralysed and then leapt up too, with no other reason than that of imitating Bamboo. Their impetus carried them out of the window and they were swallowed up. They did not return. Could they return? Maybe Bamboo would break her vows of fidelity and leave Iris behind.

I spent whole nights calling for them. The silence echoed with my cries, which fell down in the tower. All day long I looked out of the window with my hands cupped in front of my face, imitating a telescope. My plans would be impossible with a different bird or a different monkey.

I started to paint another picture, trembling with emotion rather than fear. I wanted to paint my mother, but the brushes traced ominous shapes. My curiosity at finding out how each of my paintings would end up was so great that I would never stop, even on the brink of catastrophe. The shapes I painted turned into a wizard with a hyena's face. His laugh rang out loudly when he stepped down from the canvas.

'What's your name?' he asked me.

'Luis,' I replied.

'Liar, you're called Leandro. I'm going to take you away with me in this sack.'

'And what is your name, please?' I asked him without showing any fear.

'I am called Mr Devil,' he said with a chuckle. 'Or Mr Demon, or Mr Lucifer, or Mr Satan, or Mr Luzbel alias Mandinga, et cetera, et cetera.'

'Satan? San Tan? Never heard of him. Are you in the Civil Register?'

'I have my own register.'

'But you're dressed as a woman,' I protested.

'That means nothing. I wear what I want. I can be a little boy or a giant or a gypsy or a goldfinch.'

'I don't believe that you can shrink yourself down to the size of a goldfinch.'

'I can go smaller than that. I can turn into a flea. I can be as small as a flea.'

'Impressive. I would love to see you turn into a flea. We'd need a huge theatre, with all my friends there to see you.'

The wizard, who was indeed none other than the Devil himself, was flattered by Leandro's words. He rapidly transformed himself into a flea.

'I'm going to paint a little box, the littlest box in the world, so that the biggest Devil in the world can have a place to sleep. It's a crazy trick, everyone will be just wild about it.'

Mr Devil smiled; even though it is hard to see a flea's smile, it was just visible under his dark abundant bristles.

In two minutes Leandro had painted the littlest box in the world. He painted it so well that he had no difficulty in removing it from the canvas. Once Leandro had the box in his hand, he opened the lid and the Devil got into it without any problem. So that Leandro would not be scared, the Devil, even though he had turned himself into a flea, left the lid of the box open. In order to flatter his own vanity, he started leaping out of the box and painting an audience for his great achievement. He was competing with Leandro; using the biggest brush there was, he painted a group of children from an extremely sporty school. There were girls on bicycles, carrying picnic baskets, which they immediately put down on the floor. It seemed that the tower had grown larger. Lots of the girls had very short arms and hands like rakes; lots of their bicycles had only one wheel or else oval wheels that could not turn properly.

The Devil looked at the girls joyfully, thinking of the tricks he would play on them. One of the girls had very long blonde hair, and her curls were tempting. With a single bound, the flea leapt into the space between her hair and her hairband. He was close to her neck, and could stick in his sting without difficulty. I don't know if fleas really have stings; but anyway, this flea was probably supernatural. The Devil let out a chuckle that was disproportionately loud for a flea. The crowd laughed with slight anxiety: they did not know where the chuckle had come from or if it was normal to laugh so loudly. Furious at such a reception, the Devil shut himself away in his box.

'When will this macabre party be over?' Leandro thought. 'It's a pity I don't have my pocket dictionary with me so I can look up the word macabre.'

But he remembered where he was, and opened the door quickly, let the snake through, and went to the next room. He shut himself in.

He had to be alone to be able to paint. He wanted to paint the same thing as always: his mother sitting under a tree, knitting. But unconsciously he drew a different face, the face of a boy his own age. He had often wanted to have a brother in order to share secrets or else for help in tricky situations. Now more than ever he wanted someone to help him in the difficult and dangerous adventure of finding Iris and Bamboo, for whose fates he felt responsible. Leandro thought about this the whole time he was painting the face, which ended up being frighteningly similar to his own. One might almost have thought that he was working on a self-portrait: the curly hair, the grey eyes, the eyebrows that met in the middle, the wrinkle on the forehead. A full-length portrait would take a lot of time. He worked carefully on the face for days on end. It seemed that he would never finish, but when the will is there, even the most difficult task gets finished. He had the face, but now that he was ready to paint the body, what position should he put it in? He ran to look at himself in the tower's only mirror. He leaned against the wall with his arms crossed; he crossed his legs as well and leaned a little to the right, like when he was watching people play volleyball. The figure in the painting, who was starting to move a little, was well dressed. In this he did not resemble his model very much. Leandro fitted the portrait's neck into his shirt, and made the arms of his pullover the right length. He wanted to delay the moment of bringing the painting to life because he was a little apprehensive about meeting himself. 'How stupid I was to paint myself,' he thought. He and his self-portrait greeted each other coldly.

'Hello,' one of them said.

'Hello,' the other replied.

To take their minds off things, they both went to look out of the window. Leandro put a hand to his eyes, like a visor, so he could see further.

'What are you looking for?' his double asked him.

'Iris and Bamboo.'

'Who are they?'

'Friends of mine, dear friends.'

'What country are they from?'

'I don't know.'

'Where do they live? Where do they go to school? What school do they go to?'

'They don't go to school. Bamboo is a bird and Iris is a monkey.'

When he heard this, the double laughed.

'Why are you laughing?'

'You were talking about those two as if they were humans.'

'They are humans. You can think what you want. They are humans.'

'Don't get all worked up, it was a joke.'

'I'm worried about what happened to them. I was playing with them one day and threw a paper aeroplane out of the window without meaning to.'

Leandro went up close to the window.

'You see down there? There it is, that's where they went to try to find the aeroplane, because that's how I'd taught them the game worked. I looked out of the window to see if I could see them against the ground, but it was useless. It would have been easier to find a needle or a feather. Every night I dream that I find them and that we put on a circus show together. We're very good at it. My dreams recur and get more and more successful. Bamboo flies up to perform her tricks, and Iris's imitations bring the house down. The best trick is when they rob the sweet seller and distribute his sweets to the whole audience. And there are always magically more sweets all the time.'

'Are you crying? Boys don't cry.'

'And you never cry?'

'Not for something so silly. And if you want to why don't you draw another Bamboo or another Iris?'

'They wouldn't be the same. If you've loved something very much, then nothing's ever the same.'

'But a monkey and a bird can be the same, of course they can. They're all the same.'

'You're wrong, there's lots of species, like dogs. You can have an orang-utan or a chimpanzee or a capuchin or a gorilla or a howler monkey.'

'And what about Bamboo, what species is she?'

'She's a hybrid.'

'Do you have a rope?'

'What do you want it for?'

'To go down.'

'To go down where? Don't you realise how many kilometres away the ground is?'

'What about the explorers who climb Everest and Aconcagua, eh, what about them? And for them the snow and the ice make it all even more difficult.'

'It's more dangerous to go down than to go up. Now don't distract me, I need to paint a portrait.'

'So you don't care that much about your Iris and Bamboo. Why don't you draw a rope?'

'Because the picture would just turn into a snake.'

'Well, I'll draw it, then.'

'Leave me alone.'

He needed a moment of peace in order to prepare himself to start painting again, to start painting what he wanted to paint: his mother knitting. A blank sheet of paper had fallen to the floor, and in his agitation he started to draw right there. Why could he not remember his mother clearly, if he had loved her for so long, if he had watched her until he fell asleep from watching her too much? He drew a thousand mouths as he tried to remember his mother's mouth, a thousand heads of hair as he tried to remember hers, a thousand noses, a thousand ears, a thousand necks, a thousand eyes, a thousand hands. If he managed to draw her accurately, he was sure she would immediately appear. It was this hope that inspired him to continue without pausing to eat, sleep or wash. He painted a few happy things in order to help him relax: a racing bicycle, a colour television set, a computer. Suddenly he remembered his friend: had he disappeared?

Leandro realised how hungry he was. He painted an excellent apple and a bunch of grapes, which he ate greedily. These fruits did not satisfy him so he painted a few little pies, but because he had not painted the filling they were all crust. Then he painted a sky pudding, a *budín del cielo*.

How did the sky pudding know that it came from the sky? You'd have to ask the sky. He shut his eyes and started to paint again.

Now that I've painted an apple and eaten it, now that I've painted pies and eaten them, now that I've painted a *budín del cielo* and eaten it, I'm going to paint another window, a real window with blinds and a frame, and I'm going to look out of it so I can see clearly what floor I'm on. I haven't dared find out so far. I've spent so much time wondering if I'm on the top floor or down at ground level.

I was thinking about this and I started to paint the window again. First of all I painted the edges, then the frame. While I did this I thought about how strange the window would be. It was an easy job. I finished it with a speed that was only comparable to the impatience I felt to finish it. As soon as I finished the window I leaned out of it and saw that I was, inexorably, on the highest floor of the tower, how many floors did it have anyway? I couldn't count them because it gave me vertigo to look down. What could you see from this window? The whole world. It was difficult to discern one race from another, one country from another: they were all so small and so far away. I preferred to look at the sky, which was more familiar to me. The sky that Iris and Bamboo had fallen into.

There was no one to tell him what he wanted to know: whether it was practice which led to pictures being like their subjects, and if the look in his mother's eyes would appear into the drawing as an untimely gift which he himself would not be able to explain. What he did understand, as surely as if someone had told him straight out, was that he would eventually manage to draw the exact expression in her eyes, and as he drew the delicate line of her eyelids he felt what the great artists feel, the inexplicable happiness that comes from drawing the line that you have hunted for so long and which is only just recognisable as you draw it. With a brush in his hand he looked for the right way to start setting things down. Nothing got in the way of the lines he had imagined; the fear of everything he could not see did not trouble him, neither did the fear he felt towards the things he could see: it was a quiet moment of happiness, unlike any other he had experienced since he had first come to the tower.

He set himself seriously to work. After so many attempts, the eyes he had drawn resembled his mother's eyes. He walked away from the drawing, looking at it through half-closed eyes, and was so moved that for a second he stopped work, before setting himself to colour his drawing. When he painted her hair, he thought he was making a mistake: his mother didn't have blonde curls, and she didn't hold back her hair with a metal band with sky-blue flowers; that hairstyle was the hairstyle of a little child, but he couldn't correct it. When he reached the hands, he noticed that they didn't look like an adult's hands, but rather those of a little girl. They were very pretty hands; his mother's hands were also pretty, but big people's hands couldn't be mistaken for the hands of a nine-year-old girl. But he continued working with the conviction that he would achieve the likeness that he was looking for so passionately. The dress wasn't an adult's dress either; neither were the shoes. All the clothing was wrongly chosen; as if the lines he were drawing were against his will. He reached a point when the paroxysm of concentration upset him and he threw himself onto the floor crying, but then he remembered that boys don't cry. When he got up and he looked at the painting, he was astonished: a little girl was coming gracefully out from inside the painting, and as she stepped into the tower she greeted him. It wasn't his mother, but he didn't feel much disappointment about this. He had fallen in love with the little girl he had painted by accident.

'What's your name?'

'Leandro. And yours?'

'Ifigenia.'

'That's a very portentous name. A name from history.'

'If you want, you can call me Iffi.'

'Where do you live?'

'On the beach.'

'How did you get in here?'

'I got in through a drawing that you did. I heard that you were a great painter, that you were so talented you could paint a pudding that people could really eat.'

'Who told you that?'

'A little bird.'

'What did he look like? What did he look like?'

'I don't know.'

'What's your favourite pudding?'

'Strawberry pudding.'

'If you describe it to me, maybe I'll be able to paint it.'

'It's a pink cream, like the ones ladies use for their faces.'

'There are some things that are very difficult to draw. You must choose something more common.'

'Chocolate flan.'

'That's easy, but ugly.'

'Why?'

'Because it shakes. It's a pusillanimous pudding.'

'That's because you don't paint the chocolate on top. That would hold it in place.'

'Would you prefer a flower?'

'Yes I would, if you're really good at drawing. Draw me a forget-me-not.'

'What flower is that?'

'It's called a forget-me-not.'

Next to the flower, Leandro drew a bracelet that he offered to the girl.

'I don't wear jewellery.'

'Why?'

'Jewels are nothing but worldly vanity.'

'What vanity? It's just a medical bracelet, a painkilling bracelet.'

'Pain? What pain?'

'The pains of the world. Haven't you heard about getting rheumatism when you get kicked playing rugby or fall over while ice-skating?'

'Never. The pains I know are spiritual.'

'And what is a spiritual pain, then?'

'You feel it in your heart.'

'Have you got a boyfriend?'

'Why do you ask?'

'Because you've got a ring which looks like an engagement ring.'

'Yes, this sort of ring's called an alliance, isn't it? But no, I'm never going to get married, not even for a joke.'

'Are you never going to fall in love?'

'No. I'm going to become a nun.'

'But nuns also fall in love. They fall in love with God. Anyway, I don't believe you.'

'God knows what will happen. Do you live here? Is there a lift?'

'It would have to be an infinite lift.'

Leandro, after offering her several desserts from his own paintings, showed her the abyss that was visible from the window. Ifigenia leant with a dreamy air against the window frame. She said that in her house all the windows were very boring, that you couldn't see anything, but that from this tower you could see a whole wonderful world.

'What good eyesight you have; in order to see anything I'd have to get myself a telescope.'

'You painters don't need to see very well. All they need is their imagination. I never painted. If you're a bad boy, you'll fall into this void.'

'Why would I fall?'

'Because I'll push you, to punish you.'

'Why do you want to punish me if I haven't done anything wrong? You didn't accept my bracelet, you're the one with no manners.'

'I'm going to tear up all your drawings so you can't eat any more puddings.'

'What a badly behaved girl you are.'

'I'm worse than you think, but it's all your fault: you drew me like this.'

'I didn't draw you being bad. I drew you with a pretty face.'

'A pretty face isn't enough, don't you think?'

'It must be useful for something. You could work in the cinema, or in television.'

'Perhaps, but nobody will love me just because I have a pretty face.'

'Is it very difficult for you to be a good girl?'

'It's very difficult. I can't get annoyed, I can't say bad words, I can't be disobedient, I can't tell lies, I can't laugh at people, I can't let my hair get mussed up; I have to study, I have to give away all the things I like, I have to have baths, I can't eat all the sweets I want.'

'But that's the same for everybody.'

'Yes, but I am not everybody. I'm just a drawing.'

'Please don't be bad.'

'I can dance in the air. Do you know any other girl who can do that?'

'Are you saying that because you're a drawing, you're better than other girls?'

'I'm one of your drawings, so naturally I'm worse. Isn't it a stupid idea to dance over the abyss? It's the first time that someone has drawn me. If some other person had drawn me, I don't know what I'd be like. You'll have to draw me again if you want to see me again. And what are those gloves? What are they for?'

'They're boxing gloves. You never saw boxing? Never saw it on TV?'

'It must be horrible. Are there women boxers?'

'Why must it be horrible?'

'What happens if they burst one of your eyes, or break your leg or a little finger on your hand?'

'If you know how to box nothing like that ever happens. Besides, there's always the referee.'

'Can I see how those gloves look on you? Did you bring two pairs?'

'I did, I brought them with me without planning to. One of my friends from school was going to come home and box with me. We were studying together; we had a lot of fun. And now I use the gloves as pencil cases. That's where I put my rubbers and my pencils.'

'I don't understand why it's fun. There are already enough people beating each other up without boxing. Let me see how the gloves look on you. You can wear one pair and I'll wear the other. It's difficult to put these gloves on.'

'Is there anything that isn't difficult?'

'Yeah, everything's easy apart from this. I never have any fun, but don't tell anyone. I don't have any toys, and I don't have any fun. I'm not like you, and I'm not like any one of your friends, you have to understand that.'

'That's silly. That's why you're so shy, and can't play-fight. Boxing is play-fighting. It's the noble science.'

'What I like is swimming, or showjumping, or bouncing a ball against a wall.'

'I saw a fight with my father, in Lunar Park. I came out punching the air. What had air done to me? I found out the names of all the different punches, my father taught them to me, that unforgettable afternoon. Look, I've got the gloves on. Do you like how they look on me? You should put the other ones on, so we can have a match, you and me.'

'All right, let's go. How do I stand?'

'Like this. This is how you stand on-guard.'

'How lovely. I never dreamt a game like this could exist.'

'Don't you read the newspapers? Where do you live?'

'I live wherever it is a drawing lives. I can't tell you more. This is the first bit of world I've seen, the first air I've breathed, the first sensations I've felt, the first objects I've touched. I've never known any other world or any other person.'

'And how will you live from now on? Do I need to show you the world? There isn't any time.'

'You could at least try to understand me a little better.'

'I'll try, but I don't know how I can show you everything. Look, do you see the half-moon, the crescent in the sky? That's part of the moon. In the bakery, there are things called crescents, "croissants", and you can eat them. They look a bit like bread, but they are not bread, and sometimes they have sugar on top. They are really nice. But there aren't any croissants on the moon. Do you understand?'

'No.'

'In a boxing match, it looks like boxers are killing each other; but they're fighting for friendship, for applause, to be in the newspapers, to win medals and money. Punch me. I'm not going to die.'

'OK. Like this?'

'Like that. Well done.'

'I will be the first female boxing champion. I'm pretty sure I'll be the first. I don't know any others.'

'I saw pictures of some girls boxing in the newspapers. I didn't like them.'

'My mother wouldn't like me to be a boxer. She'd say, "It's not a game for girls."'

'How do you know what your mother would say if I'm the only person you know?'

'I know myself. My mother is exactly like me. I'm sure you understand, although not everyone would. It's like boxing and "croissants" and the moon and the sun looking down on us.'

'Everything you draw becomes real? I'm curious.'

'Everything I've drawn until now, at least.'

'In that case, why don't you draw a dog or a horse and then give it to me?'

'I could do it, but I don't always draw very well.'

Leandro started drawing a dog, a very pretty dog with a red leather collar. When the dog came out of the painting, Ifigenia jumped for joy and hugged it.

'What will we call him?'

'We'll call him Love. Love because he's lovely.'

Leandro patted the dog happily.

His father had never allowed him to have a dog. To be the owner now of a dog seemed to him the greatest possible gift. Love preferred Leandro and followed him round the room. Ifigenia gave him a sweet she had in her pocket, she stroked his ear, told him secrets, but everything was useless. Disinterestedly, Love preferred Leandro, even though Leandro still hadn't given him food or drink, and still hadn't really played with him except by nudging Love with his feet. Ifigenia protested:

'It would have been better if you had drawn me a horse.'

'A horse is too big to live in a tower.'

'But there are tiny horses, very tiny ones.'

'I never know if things are going to come out tiny or enormous. It doesn't depend on me.'

'There would be space if you kept all the doors open.'

'It can't be done.'

'Why not?'

'It would be dangerous.'

'You're not very brave.'

'I am brave, but I'm not a fool. There's a spider and a snake locked in there. You laugh, but if you saw them or heard them you would be very serious.'

'What's that jangling noise?'

'What? It must be the other drawings! I didn't think they could survive in there.'

'Well, they can. Here they come, all of them, jangling their bells. Do you think we should hide?'

'There's no point. They're demons and they'll know wherever we hide.'

'Don't scare me. Some of them are very pretty.'

'They would be prettier if they didn't make so much noise.'

'There's one that looks like a harlequin, and another dressed as a doctor. There's a woman so pretty that you could spend your whole life looking at her. Don't fall in love, please.'

'I'll never fall in love with anyone, if it's not you.'

'That's not true, liar.'

'It is true.'

'Here they come now. One of them is getting close to me.'

And the demon spoke: 'Who lives in this tower?'

'Well, I'm here. But I don't really know who else lives here, because all the doors are locked.'

'I've got a special key that opens all doors. It's called a master key.'

'I won't believe it until I see it.'

'Does it look like all the keys put together? Does it open all the doors? Show it to me. Give it to me.'

'He's right, you should open something soon so I believe you, because they told me that all of you are liars. If you sell brushes, they don't brush; if you sell combs, they don't comb; if you sell matches, they don't light up; if you sell sweets, they're bitter; if you sell a Christmas cake, it's not a real Christmas cake; if you sell a beautiful necklace, it breaks as soon as you put it on, and the stones keep rolling all over the floor until the Last Judgement.'

'What's the Last Judgement?' Leandro asked.

'Don't you know?' the demon said. 'It's the last day of all life, when God judges men to decide whether they go to heaven or to hell.'

'Where will you go? Heaven or hell?'

'Heaven, most probably. The jangling of our bells is the most beautiful sound in the whole world.'

'I'm not so sure. It's a devilish sound. It makes me woozy so I don't even know where I am. I am a good girl, you should know. It's possible to see the goodness in people's eyes, and let me tell you that as soon as I hear your jangling noise it makes me want to renounce goodness.'

'Oh, come on,' said the demon. 'Don't think badly of me. I'm exactly like all boys and girls in the world. You've seen me opening this door.'

'The key is so stiff it doesn't work. But don't get annoyed with it.'

'Here we go, here we go. The key works! It's open!' The key turned a little and the demon spoke triumphantly.

Seeing the chicken-spider, Ifigenia pushed everyone except Leandro into the room and locked the door on them.

'I think I'll leave the tower soon,' she said. 'It's dangerous. There are very strange people appearing all the time, and one doesn't know how to behave with them. There are supernatural beings who jangle bells, who open all doors with a master key, even though I've got that now. Really, it's impossible to get any sleep here.'

'As long as I watch the door to each room, you'll be able to sleep soundly. You shouldn't get angry for silly reasons. Please, don't threaten to go and leave me all alone.'

'I'm not threatening you, but I have a dog and a cat at home waiting for me. Who's going to feed them? There's only me, because no one else loves them like I do.'

'If they loved you, they'd have come with you.'

'They couldn't come. They would have done if that had been possible.'

'Don't cry.'

'I'm not crying, but I've got a lump in my throat. How do you think people manage not to cry?'

'You take a deep breath.'

'Teach me how.'

'Breathe. Hold your breath. Well, since you asked me, I will draw you a horse.'

Leandro started painting a horse, but Love stopped his hand by putting his little paw on the canvas. Each time Leandro started drawing again, Love used his paws to prevent him from continuing. Ifigenia, impatient, was trying to distract the dog, who kept insisting by putting his little paw on the canvas, where Leandro had only managed to draw the outline of a horse's ear.

'Never, you'll never be able to give me a little horse!' Ifigenia cried out. 'Love doesn't love me!'

Leandro, desperate, said to her:

'It doesn't depend on me.'

'Let's lock Love in the other room,' Ifigenia suggested.

'I wouldn't like to do that.'

'Then you don't love me.'

'I love you a lot, but I don't want Love to suffer because of that.'

'Just for a minute. In one minute you could do the painting.'

Hearing these words, Love pressed himself against the door and there was no force or cajoling that could make him move. Leandro used this moment to draw the little horse, but it didn't look like a little horse, it looked like a marsupial. The horse didn't move inside the canvas but stayed still, waiting to be called. Because of his tiger-like pelt, they called him Tiger. All they had to do was to call his name out loud for him to start moving. He gave a jump and landed softly on the floor, like in a circus. Ifigenia patted his neck and whispered something into his ear, but she didn't want to get on his back. Leandro said that she should trot around the room.

'I'm scared,' she said.

'It's not very far to fall.'

'But I'd be scared and I would fall. He is so small. There are no horses this small.'

'Why did you make me draw a little horse, then? If it had been big, you'd have said it was too big to be locked in a room. Now that it's small you're scared of it. You're scared of everything and you are ungrateful. I wasted my time drawing this horse. I'm very busy with a very important portrait I'm trying to do.'

'You can do whatever you want. I don't need you to look after me.'

'Well, I'm very glad of that, because otherwise we'd end up having a whole zoo in the tower. Next time you would ask me to draw a cat, a rabbit, or who knows what. Who knows if you wouldn't ask me to draw an elephant or a giraffe or an orang-utan.'

'I will go and take Tiger away with me. He will follow me. But he's not a horse, he's a marsupial. Can't you see the belly he has? I hope your portrait comes out all right. Can you say who you are painting?'

'My mother.'

'Is she pretty?'

'Of course she's pretty, and she's very good.'

'Will you show me the portrait?'

'If it comes out right.'

'You were very sure earlier that it was going to come out right.'

'Sometimes I'm so scared it won't that I cry.'

'Scared?'

'Scared that it won't look like her.'

'Don't worry, you'll be fine. Please don't punish Tiger just because he can't gallop. Where is the toilet?'

'For who, for Tiger?'

'Not Tiger, me. I want to wash my hands and comb my hair.'

They went into the bathroom with Tiger following them. It was a sky-blue and green room. Three different types of toilet paper were winding down from above. There wasn't any bath, only a shower, held in place by little devils who invited anyone who looked at them to come and try the water, and who poured freezing or boiling water from their mouths. The toilet itself was beautiful, you had to climb a ladder in order to sit at it.

All those things, so shiny and pleasant, ended up disappointing them. They saw the three coloured papers that furled down from above suddenly become entangled with one another and stop rolling down. When the rolls were touched, even very lightly, the machinery made a very unpleasant screeching noise, and there was no human skill that could grasp a single sheet of paper. The shower, held in place by the lovely devils who invited anyone who looked at them to come and try the water, was almost dangerous. The water was so cold that it turned into stalactites when it fell onto your body, or else so hot that it burned your skin. The picturesque toilet, the one you could only get to by climbing a quaint set of stairs, shook whenever anyone tried to sit comfortably on it. Ifigenia washed her hands in a blue basin, with a tablet of soap that looked like a jewel; she had chosen it from a selection of various soaps exhibited in little baskets, but the light shining from this jewel stained her hands violently red. When she chose the prettiest towel of all the ones on offer, the one with little hands painted on it, and tried to use it to dry her face, she felt the little hands, which had started out by stroking her, start to pinch her, and left her face and her hands greasy. When she finished combing her hair with a musical comb that had really caught her fancy, she noticed that the comb had actually been pulling out her hair.

Ifigenia, who was a very well brought-up girl, did not complain but merely put on her nicest smile and spoke to Leandro:

'Could I go into the kitchen? I'm hungry and thirsty.'

'Hungry, after I painted you so many puddings?'

'Man cannot live by pudding alone.'

They entered the kitchen, where there was a robot that fed anybody who dared to experiment with things they had never tried before. Hanging from the sky like tropical fruits there was an infinite number of desserts; some of them pretended to be clouds of pink and white cream, just hanging in the air; the little pots of ice cream, with a sea painted on the wall for background, had little spoons that acted as oars. The hens waiting to be put into the oven had hats with cherries on them; the capons were turning on a strange mechanism, wearing dinner jackets. There was no beef, or fish; there were lots of greens and lettuce. But all the possible combinations of ingredients that promised a Pantagruelian banquet hid horrible surprises. The desserts were as hard as marble; the tropical fruits were a swarm of flies; the pink and white creams that were trying to be clouds were only painted foam; the hens with the straw hats with cherries on them were impossible to put into the oven or the pot because they pecked viciously at any hand that came close to them: instead of you eating the hen, the hen ate you. The capons in the dinner jackets smoked continuously, and this vice did not allow them to take a break long enough to get cooked; the lettuce was made of paper.

Faced with this, Ifigenia took a pink ice cream, and Tiger took three white ones; one for him and two for his two sons. Ifigenia said farewell: 'I have to go.' She took a couple of dancing steps in mid-air and, laughing, disappeared through the window.

Leandro sighed. His new task was to draw an automobile. He searched his memory for all the automobiles he had really liked, especially the racing ones. He liked the most modern automobiles, but if he found his mother, then a low-slung car wouldn't be comfortable for her. He imagined it as being a lustrous green. The beauty of a car consists particularly in its speed; the next most important thing is suspension, or perhaps the litres of naphtha it consumes, or its oil consumption, because life has become very expensive. Last of all we need to consider the power of its motor. He would have to look for the sort of automobile he could take out for little spins. A racing automobile would be a caprice, and the price of automobiles means we shouldn't be capricious about them. Even if it didn't cost him anything, he would have to spend money on its upkeep.

While he was drawing it, he felt a little worried. What happened to me with the little horse is a bad experience. Instead of drawing a little horse I drew a marsupial. How could I have got it so wrong? True, there are animals that look like each other, but there was never any likeness between a horse and a kangaroo. I'm scared to draw an automobile that ends up being a lizard. They would be as fast as each other, but who could travel in a lizard?

Leandro started drawing on a piece of paper. He was in such a hurry that he grabbed the closest thing to hand: coloured pencils. He started with the chassis and the wheels, continued with the bonnet and the doors. He didn't forget the colour green, the colour of hope. His hope increased with each stroke, each line he drew. It wasn't the first time he had drawn an automobile. After karate class, he used to draw automobiles endlessly. He had also drawn them on the walls with green chalk when he was walking back from school, the same colour green as he was now using for his drawing. It is difficult to concentrate; sometimes, one doesn't concentrate most on what one really wants to concentrate on. The drawing was perfect. Leandro thought that he had finished it, but something must have been missing, since it didn't become real. It's true that it had no headlights or windscreen wipers, no rear-view mirror, no tyre-pump, no jack, no toolkit, no spare tyre, no seatbelts... Could that be the reason why it didn't start up? If it wasn't real, it couldn't start up. And how could he start it if he didn't have the keys? How humiliating for a creator not to have foreseen all these problems! He put this task to one side and, disappointed, went to look for the portrait of his mother. Love, who was a guard dog, was next to the portrait. What danger could he be protecting it from? As if he were trying to point something out, Love whined, and gave a little bark. It was his first bark.

With the automobile in front of him and almost finished, he paused before getting in and sitting at the wheel. After checking that none of the keys he had with him fitted the lock, he leaned with his arms on the wheel and put his head into his arms. Anyone would have thought that he was crying. Whose sympathy was he fishing for? He was alone. Or were there people gathering on the other side of the door: animals, ophidians, a pretty girl, a devil, a nice boy? Perhaps solitude was best for what he was intending to do next. And what about the automobile, which he had put so much hope into drawing? Would it disappoint him and transform into a turtle? How would he make the motor run? Where would he get horsepower, h.p.? Why hadn't I studied mechanics when that chauffeur kept inviting me to work in his garage? My father would have punished me, and in order to avoid a punishment I denied myself the chance of learning what would have saved my automobile. When will I, how will I ever become the owner of an automobile? A real one, not a toy one like all the ones I've had up till now? A brilliant idea came into my mind: to draw a mechanic and his toolbox. I grabbed my drawing paper. This time I sat in the driving seat.

He started to draw the mechanic. He did it quickly: he was tall, perhaps too tall, with a little black moustache, long curly hair, penetrating large eyes, and a long oval face, something which contrasted with his eccentric dress. When he finished the drawing, Leandro realised that the mechanic was much too tall.

'Can I be of some assistance? Do you need anything?' asked the mechanic, trying to look less tall than he was.

'My automobile won't start up. The clutch and the accelerator don't work.'

'How long have you had this problem?'

'How should I know? I've only had this automobile since today.'

'In that case, would you like me to check the motor?'

'Whatever you think best.'

The mechanic opens the bonnet, checks the motor, but says nothing. He tries to get the automobile to start with a key he has in his pocket, but it's useless. Suddenly he stops dead.

'What's wrong?' asked Leandro.

'I just feel faint. Where are the keys?'

Leandro moves away, and with a scrap of paper and a pencil, he leans against the automobile's door and draws a key. He takes it out of the paper and tries it in the lock.

'What shall we do? Don't you have a little trolley so I can look at it from underneath?'

'There's one in the next room.'

The mechanic leaves the room and comes back bringing the trolley. When he passes through the door he hits his head on the frame, he stumbles, he reaches the automobile staggering, he slips the trolley underneath the car and lies down on it.

'What's happening? Did you hit yourself very badly? Do you want me to call a doctor?'

'Call one, yes, call one.'

With great skill, Leandro draws a doctor carrying his doctor's bag. The doctor asks:

'Anybody hurt?'

'I don't know,' answers Leandro. 'He hit his head and felt faint.'

'Let's see,' says the doctor. He takes a sphygmomanometer out of his bag. 'It's nothing. Just a fright. A mishap. You'll feel better soon.'

'I must take the car to the garage and I don't feel up to it. I feel very faint,' said the mechanic.

'I feel faint, I feel faint… you hardly hit yourself. What would you do in a race?'

'I would drive just like all the others.'

'Not like the others, no. I know someone who drove himself out of a window.'

'How did he do it? Was he Batman?'

'No, just someone who didn't frighten easily.'

'Well then let's see, since you say you're a hero. What are you going to do to get out?'

'We'll put some pieces of wood at the window, to make a ramp.'

'But don't you see we're very high up?'

The mechanic brings some pieces of wood. He gets into the back seat of the car. The doctor sits at the wheel and manages to start the motor.

'I have my own parachute,' explains the doctor.

The car starts up and disappears through the window.

Will they bring my car back? I don't have the address of either the doctor or the mechanic. I will never forget that car. It was mine and it looked like a car out of a dream. My automobile, the nicest one in all Buenos Aires. When will I find another one if this one doesn't come back? If it doesn't come back… my dog would come back if I whistled for him.

I will write a letter to Ifigenia. How will I send it to her? I suppose everything is possible if you really want it.

*My beloved Ifigenia:*

*In order not to lose it, I am wearing the bracelet I will give to you; the fact that I do this should tell you that since you left I have done nothing else apart from think about your eyes, which are nearly the same colour as the bracelet. How empty the world now looks without your words, inside the tower's loneliness, the silence of its windows. To have known you in such an environment seems to me unreal, like being in a movie. When I move, I feel as if I was in a cartoon, filled with nostalgia. I haven't eaten any dessert since you left; they all seem the same to me now, with the same icing, with the same consistency, with the same taste. They all taste of tears. Tiger left following you; if it were possible, I would imitate him like a dog. When I am old, if I marry you, I will be the director of a zoological garden, with tame animals, and you will help me to teach them the ABC for exams. All the exercises they perform will have background music and when they give me back my automobile I will drive you around the world pulling a caravan behind us where we will sleep and eat. In each village we will perform with all the animals. We won't take a circus tent, as there'll be room enough for us to sleep in the caravan. What do you say to that?*

*How shall I send you this letter? Many things seem impossible, but they happen if one really wishes them to do so. I will find a way to make this letter reach your hands, even if no carrier pigeons or helicopters appear round here to pick up the post.*

*I await your answer anxiously and remain, kissing your feet. Accept the bracelet the colour of your eyes.*

*Leandro*

Since I didn't get a reply, I wrote to her again.

*Dear Ifigenia:*
*I've thought about you so much that I can't imagine anything apart from your face. I draw it desperately, but instead of your eyes I draw other eyes, and I am scared that you will come out of the painting transformed into a different person. I can't remember the oval of your face, or your pretty hands. I get confused, I get disturbed, my thoughts get cloudy because I don't know how to avoid this fear that seizes hold of me whenever I draw your mouth or your lips. Your mouth is what I prefer in your face, and indeed is the part I like best in everyone's face. It makes me suffer, to see your mouth before it is completely drawn, when there is still the unremembered bit to draw, your under-lip that pouts over your upper lip. I think I don't know anything better than I know your face, but since I've started to draw it I can't stop myself from adding features that don't belong to it. How will I continue with this painting which does not look like you, where the hair is the wrong colour, or the part-open lips are the wrong shape? My God, I don't think I'd be able to cope with anyone who wasn't you. It's my fault, but I don't think I'd be able to look at her in the eyes like I look at you. I hate this devilish tower! I wish that the world would quickly transform itself, that the stars in the sky would fall, or that somebody would switch off the lights so I don't have to see you any more. Now that I've finished my new portrait, I think I will be able to lie on the floor and sleep, at least if the person that I draw doesn't come close to me and conquer me like you conquered me. I have finished, and I will send you this*

*letter through the air. Ifigenia, please, never forget me. I am the saddest of people in this badly drawn tower. Never forget me.*

*Leandro*

The new girl Leandro had drawn came out of the painting.

'What's your name?' he asked when he saw her.

'Alice in Wonderland.'

He looked at her and said: 'I really should make some changes to you. I don't like the shape of your face, or your mouth, or your eyes; I don't like the way you're looking at me. Please, get back into the frame. I will make a few changes, but before I do tell me something nice that I can remember.'

'I would like you to take me far away, deep down to the bottom of the sea.'

'I will draw you surrounded by shells and water and waves, and you will swim with the waves and go to the deepest part of the sea.'

Alice gets back into the frame and transforms; she jumps and leaps through the window, waving goodbye.

*Dear Alice in Wonderland:*

*I write to you without much hope. I don't think this letter will ever get into your hands. If you pass close to this window, you will see the envelope addressed to you and then you will stop walking. Perhaps then you will read my letter and find out that since I met you I haven't done anything apart from think of you. I keep drawing you with all my soul, I put all my wit to the service of drawing you, because only this way will you appear again like on that beautiful day when I met you. The sun was shining in every corner of the tower, but it wasn't the sun that lit us up, but you with your great big eyes. I thought it was a dream, and that you would be different. How wrong I was! Now I understand that my mistake was a test, and that I have to fight to see you again.*

*I have in my hands a pencil with which to draw you. For lack of time, I didn't choose the best pencil, but the first one that came to hand... I am trying with all my might to draw you exactly as you are. I would like you to understand that you are different from all the other girls I have ever seen, and that even if it were possible to say that you looked like yourself, you wouldn't then be the girl I met, so different are you from all others. Please, help me draw you. Don't allow other faces to get in the way and make me forget your face. I need to see your face in order to draw it. When I was small I couldn't draw very well and everything looked wrong. People didn't like the way I drew my proportions. Now there's no one to tell me that this is wrong, that you are different, much more beautiful and seductive, and that the pencil in my desperate hand is shaking. I beg you, help me with all your wisdom and I will be able to paint a portrait so good that it would be exhibited in any museum. I know I sound pretentious, but I am not. You must know that it is love that makes me pretentious. I am going to draw a sledge to come and find you. You will object that there is no snow, but I plan to draw the snow too. I will sketch lines that I have never drawn before. I think I'm on the right track. The sledge looks like all other sledges, and the snow like all snow. Would you like to come into the sledge with me? I will add in the reindeer who will pull the sledge, but before all that I must draw you carefully. The mouth is the hardest thing. How difficult the ears and neck and hands are as well. Where will I put them? What will your expression be? I propose to do something very, very hard. So many things! I don't know if I will be able to achieve them all. I'm not a great painter, really, not even a great draughtsman, some might say that I've never painted in my whole life. Don't look down on me, Alice. Isn't it possible that I can't draw well because of you? Isn't it possible that you have disturbed me? You didn't make me lose faith in myself. I was never in the middle of a snowy landscape, I've never seen reindeer, I've never seen sledges, I've never seen you sitting in a sledge, wrapped in furs like a Russian woman, or a Chinese woman, or an Eskimo.*

*I've got an idea. I know how to make kites. A boy from school taught me how to make a six-sided one, very pretty. In my bag I have just the kind of paper you need for it, and the twine, and the sticks, and the ribbons for the tail. Now that there are so many planes and helicopters, it seems silly to build a form of transport as simple as a kite; but the advantage is that I know very well how to draw one. I have metres and metres of cord. I will draw us a mermaid, in case it falls into the sea. Mermaids can swim, and she will take your letters as well. For greater security, I will send my letter in a bottle. I told you once that if we were ever separated without being able to communicate with each other,*

*I would send you my letter inside a bottle, but probably you will not remember this, because you are a very modern girl and probably think that a message cannot travel in a bottle but instead has to go via telegrams and so on.*

*Goodbye, Alice. I can't draw you. I've lost you.*
*Leandro*

The first thing I saw entering the room where I was working on my mother's portrait was the portrait itself, broken on the floor. I stopped dead. Nothing could have hurt me more. I went closer, without thinking about what I was doing, I knelt down to touch the canvas and see if anything was missing, but everything was missing: I didn't recognise what used to be the painting, I could only see the background with the green foliage. I understood immediately who had ruined the painting. The stains of the little paws, the claws and teeth revealed only one possible culprit: the dog. What is more, the fact that the dog had disappeared was highly significant. Where was he? Where was he hiding? I called him peremptorily. No one appeared. I searched in every corner. I was choking with indignation. I thought about punishing him. I had to punish him. How? I would make a whip with knotted cords, something I had learned about from a magazine. I drew it. It had three knots. I finished drawing it in a fury. I swished it through the air to hear it crack. I went around the corridors of the tower in a frenzy, forgetting about spiders and snakes, hitting whatever crossed my path with the whip, all the time shouting 'Love, Love!' in different voices, trying to conquer him, to terrify him, to threaten him. Finally when there was no hope left I came close to the window to look out at the day, and I saw that Love was coming towards the tower with his head down, his legs bent, repentant. Love had one virtue: if he was sad he bent like a ball of wool, he almost disappeared. I felt touched. The noise of the whip through the air died away. Love knew very well what he had done, and threw himself at my feet. I couldn't say anything, and was ashamed and hid the whip underneath a chair. I felt guilty because I hadn't thought about the painting for a long time, I had spent all my time thinking about Ifigenia and Alice. I bent my head as well, and when Love put his own head on my lap, half-closing his eyes, I stroked him. No apology was ever sweeter.

With determination I started painting the ill-fated portrait again. I never worked with such eagerness, such submission to my task, such desperation. For hours I painted without a break, with half-closed eyes, approaching the canvas, stepping back. I prayed out loud for God to hear me, because my last chance to ever see my mother again depended on this drawing. Night and day I worked without stopping, until an intense light seemed to illuminate the sky and against the sky my drawing, this likeness of my mother that had been so difficult to obtain, became radiant, so radiant that I couldn't look at it directly without shading my exhausted eyes. But when will my mother congratulate me, make that loving gesture so different from all others?

Waiting is difficult, but not even the Devil could prevent me from seeing her again. Everything he could try would be useless.

The inside of the tower was silent. Where could the bicycles be, the little girls with their bent faces, the spider, the snake, the Devil? Perhaps the Devil is not as powerful as we think, for if he were, then he would have come out of the little box already and opened the door. Is the Devil really as important as we think?

They always spoke badly about him to me. The strangest thing is that in carnival they always wanted to dress me as a devil. I realised it was for economic reasons. It's the cheapest costume there is. It's completely red. You can make his claws with those flowers, you know, sweetpeas, you can paint the moustache with a burnt cork, and the horns and the little jangling bells are cheap.

Leandro came close to the window, with a pencil and paper in his hand. He had to draw something, something very important that he didn't quite understand, so disturbed he was by the latest occurrences: the sudden disappearance of Ifigenia, the arrival of the doctor and the mechanic and, more disturbing than all the rest, the impetuous exit of the automobile through the window. Where would they be now? He checked his watch for the first time since he had arrived in the tower. It had never occurred to him that he could check the time. He brought it close to his ear, and heard with emotion that it was still ticking. Nine o'clock, the little hands said. He leant against the window-frame and, standing there leaning into the air as he was, he started drawing an object, the most fantastical object in the world that he could remember: a pair of high-quality binoculars. It was hard to remember the labyrinth of those two tunnels that contained the lenses, it was hard to remember the mechanisms which advance and retract the mirrors, the little mechanical wheels, which also focus the image. Impressed by his drawing's accuracy, he leaned back over the frame of the window and contemplated with such relish the lines he had drawn that for an instant he forgot the reason he had drawn them. It seemed to him as faithful and precise as one of Leonardo da Vinci's drawings, and it was completely finished. He extracted the high-quality binoculars from the paper. He looked through them as normal; next, he turned them round and looked again. He saw everything far away and very small, very very small. He focussed the lenses. He looked eagerly through the window to the outside world, up and down. He looked at the horizon, staring as far as he could, so far that when the moment came he could hardly make out his own mother. Tiny, tiny, she was approaching, crossing a huge bridge, which was the distance between her and his eyes. She was coming closer but it was as if she were walking away, as if she were following a star. He could hardly see her, but it was her, no doubt about it, only she was so tiny she could have been his own daughter. His mother didn't make any sign to show that she could see him but no sign was necessary. Leandro knew that she was seeing him as he was seeing her. Crossing any distance, crossing any silence; thanks to his high-quality binoculars, so perfect that they looked like one of Leonardo da Vinci's inventions, but which he himself had drawn in order to see her, even if it were a tiny version of her, and to go to her side.

In his joy, Leandro leant thoughtlessly out of the window and suddenly the binoculars fell from his hands. He tried to stop them falling, he cried out, it was too late.

He felt sorry not to have remembered to draw a strap, such as people have for real binoculars and cameras.

*Dear Alice:*
*How strange the world will seem to me when I get home, if I ever get home. I will recognise the entrance to my house, the trees in the garden whose names my mother taught me, the buddleia with its strange flowers, the dark green jasmine leaves, the jasmine flowers themselves, the blossom, some white, some yellow; the magnolia flowers so high in the trees I used to climb in order to gather a bouquet to sell in the street, but which unfailingly withered and whose petals turned dark brown; the little stones along the path which went round the house and which were so well raked by the gardener who came once a week to prune and water the plants. Could it be possible that mother is waiting for me? There are days in which everything seems possible. Today is one of those days. I still have chocolates in my pocket; some of them are completely melted. This is how I like them best: a chocolate cream in silver paper. After eating it I lick the paper. Without the silver paper I wouldn't like chocolate. The flavour is all in the wrapping. Still, it would be silly to buy chocolates simply because of the silver paper. It's the same thing with people. One loves them for certain physical attributes, although this is not something you could tell everybody. Some days I feel attracted by a girl in a sky-blue dress. I wouldn't like the same girl if she were dressed in black. Perhaps because I'm a boy I'm a little bit frivolous. I hope to correct this very soon. If someone were to ask*

*me what the thing is that I would like to possess most in the world, I would answer: an automobile. Not a big, one but rather a tiny one, very tiny, so I could travel all over the world, with a circus tent in the boot where the extra wheel is meant to go. I would put it up every night to go to sleep. In this topless tower I never felt sleepy. It's the only advantage to being here. It would be very nice to go to other places together. Would you travel with me? But how will I get this letter to you? I beg you, you must explain it to me now, while you move away, or disappear, which wings I must wear to fly and reach you.*

Will the images we've seen throughout our lives remain inside our eyes? Will we be like a modern camera, filled with little rolls of film; of course, rolls that don't require to be developed? If I die before reaching my home, before seeing my mother whom I love so much, will she get to see the photographic film stored inside me? Will she see everything I did in this horrible tower that belongs to the Devil? I hope I look good in the pictures, and that mother thinks that my hair looks nice and my clothes are clean, even if that's not exactly the case.

Later, he thought that perhaps he would manage to be part of the history of photography: the first child who took pictures without a camera and who developed them without a darkroom. He tried not to be vain, but he was happy about the idea of becoming famous.

The silence was perfect. He could only hear the crickets, the birds, the noise of the sun rising (whenever the sun did rise). These were good moments to work. Leandro applied himself to painting his mother's portrait. He thought he would never finish it. He felt relieved without the binoculars, even though he had regretted their loss so much to start with. Suddenly he saw his mother coming out of the picture. She was coming out to kiss him. At that very moment, the whole tower crumbled down. Amongst the beautiful dissolving ruins, only Love appeared, because the dog had followed him with the same joy that we feel at the end of a nightmare and at the magical beginning of a piece of creative work.

The garden appeared, with its flowers, its hammocks, with its birdsong, with its pines and cedars.

In the distance, Leandro saw his mother picking something up from amongst the ruins.

'Leandro! Where were you? I've been looking for you.'

'It's me who was looking for you. What's this?'

Leandro picked up a piece of glass from the floor and showed it to his mother.

'It's from a painting. A moment ago it fell from the wall where I had hung it. But don't touch it, you could hurt yourself.'

'Did you buy it from that man who came to sell you paintings, Mr San Tan?

'That's right.'

'And is he still around here?'

'When these ruins fell, I heard a strange noise in the garden. That man appeared, he waved his hand in the distance and shouted out: "See you very soon!"'

Mother took a twig brush to sweep up the broken glass.

'Let me help you. You always do too much.'

'How changed you are! Where did you learn to be such a good boy?'

'Oh, I've learned a great many things.'

'Like what?'

'That the Devil is not so devilish. That insects and reptiles are not so bad, that drawing is not so hard, that falling in love is beautiful, that there's nothing quite as good as having friends, that happiness exists, and sometimes happiness has the face of a dog. That being brave means being scared but not paying attention to it, not caring about the fear. That being locked in a tower can be almost fun; that writing keeps memories alive, and that seeing one's mother again is the greatest happiness of all.'

'You've learnt a lot. Who taught you all this? Which books did you read? Which tower are you talking about? Who have you met?'

'I've met Love.'

'Who is he? Where is he?'

'He's lying at your feet.'

One day I will rescue my paintings. I think that somewhere in the world, I will find the tower in which they are locked away. I'm not scared of anything, not even the Devil. I'm brave, and my tale has some missing images that are still in the tower. And my dog? How is it possible he followed me? Is it possible that a dog remains faithful even in a drawing? I cup my hands round my mouth: 'Love, Love!' I hear his footsteps. I kneel down to say hello to him. The dog is here.

## Biographical note

Silvina Ocampo was born in Buenos Aires in 1903, the youngest of six children in an elite Argentine family. Silvina's eldest sister, Victoria, later became an author and founder of *Sur* magazine and is remembered as one of Argentina's great cultural figures. Educated at home, Silvina would later study drawing in Paris. Ocampo's literary career began with the publication in 1937 of her first book of short stories, *Viaje olvidado* (*The Forgotten Journey*), but it would be eleven years until the next volume of prose writing would appear in the form of *Autobiografía de Irene* (*Irene's Autobiography*) published in 1948. During the intervening years, however, Ocampo published three volumes of award-winning poetry, *Enumeración de la patria*, *Espacios métricos* and *Los sonetos del jardín*. Throughout the rest of her life, Ocampo would continue to write both poetry and short stories; she is in particular remembered today for her numerous children's stories.

During the 1930s, she scandalised even her inner circle when she took the much younger Adolfo Bioy Casares first as her lover and, later, her husband. Following her marriage to Bioy Casares in 1940, Ocampo collaborated with her husband and their close friend, Jorge Luis Borges, on two literary anthologies. In contrast to many of those around her who became national icons of their generation, Ocampo remained suspicious of journalists throughout her life, and refused to participate in the more public aspects of a writer's career. In 1954, following Bioy Casares' death, Ocampo adopted his daughter Marta.

Among several literary awards earned throughout her literary career, Silvina Ocampo was awarded the National Prize for Poetry in 1962. She died in her native Buenos Aires in 1993. Her work has been translated into French, German, English and Italian.

## HESPERUS PRESS

Hesperus Press is committed to bringing near what is far – far both in space and time. Works written by the greatest authors, and unjustly neglected or simply little known in the English-speaking world, are made accessible through new translations and a completely fresh editorial approach. Through these classic works, the reader is introduced to the greatest writers from all times and all cultures.

For more information on Hesperus Press, please visit our website: **www.hesperuspress.com**

**NEW AND FORTHCOMING TITLES FROM HESPERUS WORLDWIDE**

| Author | *Title* | *Foreword writer* |
|---|---|---|
| Eduardo Belgrano Rawson | *Washing Dishes in Hotel Paradise* | |
| Buddhadeva Bose | *My Kind of Girl* | |
| Bankim Chandra Chatterjee | *The Forest Woman* | |
| Shiro Hamao | *The Devil's Disciple* | |
| Kanoko Okamoto | *A Riot of Goldfish* | David Mitchell |
| Rabindranath Tagore | *Boyhood Days* | Amartya Sen |
| Rabindranath Tagore | *Farewell Song* | |

## SELECTED TITLES FROM HESPERUS PRESS

| Author | *Title* | *Foreword writer* |
| --- | --- | --- |
| M. Ageyev | *A Romance with Cocaine* | Toby Young |
| Mary Borden | *The Forbidden Zone* | Malcolm Brown |
| Rupert Brooke | *Letters from America* | Benjamin Markovits |
| Anthony Burgess | *The Eve of St Venus* | |
| Ivy Compton-Burnett | *Pastors and Masters* | Sue Townsend |
| Walter de la Mare | *Missing* | Russell Hoban |
| E.M. Forster | *The Obelisk* | Amit Chaudhuri |
| Graham Greene | *No Man's Land* | David Lodge |
| Aldous Huxley | *After the Fireworks* | Fay Weldon |
| Mikhail Kuzmin | *Wings* | Paul Bailey |
| Jack London | *The People of the Abyss* | Alexander Masters |
| Klaus Mann | *Alexander* | Jean Cocteau |
| Luigi Pirandello | *Loveless Love* | |
| Vita Sackville-West | *The Heir* | |
| Leonardo Sciascia | *A Simple Story* | Paul Bailey |
| Frank Wedekind | *Mine-Haha* | |
| Edith Wharton | *Fighting France: from Dunkerque to Belfort* | Colm Tóibín |
| Leonard Woolf | *A Tale Told by Moonlight* | Victoria Glendinning |
| Virginia Woolf | *Memoirs of a Novelist* | |
| Yevgeny Zamyatin | *We* | Alan Sillitoe |